Lori & Alan,

Thank You for Your support.

Merry Christmas & God Bless!

Hugs & Nickers

10-18-14

A CHRISTMAS RESCUE

BY

FREDERICK G. MARENGO

ILLUSTRATED BY

Carolyn S. Kubiak

Published by

American History Press

Free Spirit Books

an imprint of

American History Press

Staunton, Virginia

(888) 521-1789

Visit us on the Internet at:

www.Americanhistorypress.com

ISBN 13: 978-1-939995-05-6

Library of Congress Control Number: 2014949853

October 2014

Manufactured in the United States of America on acid-free paper.

This book meets all ANSI standards for archival quality.

ACKNOWLEDGEMENTS

To GOD who gave me back my health.

To my wife Susan, who is a true Christmas Carole. Many thanks for your love and encouragement that put A Christmas Rescue on bookshelves.

My deep appreciation to David Kane of American History Press for making a dream come true.

A special thank you to Santa Claus for reminding us that we must Believe.

A

CHRISTMAS RESCUE

A

CHRISTMAS RESCUE

Chapter 1

*T*he worldwide reindeer flu epidemic was first discovered in northern Finland in the middle of December and spread out of control to the herds in Siberia. The virus continued across the frozen tundra, infecting the reindeer herds all the way to the North Pole. The reindeer were fatigued, had upset stomachs and respiratory difficulty. They just wanted to burrow and sleep in the snow caves that they had created in the deep snow until they were better. The landscape was peppered with thousands of antlers protruding above the snowy terrain, but there were no reindeer in sight. They were fast asleep in their snowy hideaways. Yes, even Santa's reindeer were in a deep slumber in the reindeer barn.

An emergency worldwide conference of experts in veterinary medicine had been convened at the United Nations in New York City to come up with a plan to halt the flu virus before it reached Santa Claus's reindeer herd, but alas, it was too late. The flu would just have to run its course. There would be no toys for the children of the world, unless there was a miracle.

Rudolph's normally bright red nose now only cast a dim glow in Santa's reindeer barn, barely illuminating the sleeping eight reindeer. Dasher, Dancer, Prancer, Vixen, Comet, Cupid, Donner and Blitzen were dozing in

their stalls, flu bug stricken.

Santa called his Elves together at the North Pole Elf Education Academy to see what ideas they might have to get all the toys delivered on Christmas Eve.

What other animal could fly across the sky after being sprinkled with magic flying powder? It would have to be an animal that was powerful, graceful, and intelligent. One elf suggested a cow, another suggested a camel, and still another suggested a pig, but none of these animals could duplicate the beauty and grace of the reindeer. The Elves sat scratching their heads, trying to think of an animal that could take the place of Santa's reindeer, when Mrs. Claus joined the conversation. She said that she had a suggestion. All eyes turned to her, as they waited breathlessly for a solution to their dilemma. "You want an animal that is powerful, graceful and intelligent? I am surprised that you didn't think of this animal at once. There is only one choice, of course. It must be a horse."

Cheers sounded through the air and the elves danced with joy. Santa was filled with glee, as he gave Mrs. Claus a big hug. "Yes! Yes! The horse must be the animal that saves Christmas."

He immediately said to Alfred, his chief computer elf, "The horses must not only be powerful, graceful and intelligent, but also *happy*. After all, this is the happiest time of the entire year. Go to work Alfred, and hurry! We are almost out of time, since Christmas Eve is fast approaching. Not only must you find suitable horses, but we have to make certain the magic flying powder that you sprinkle on them will enable them to soar through the air with all of the beauty and grace of my reindeer."

Alfred hurried to the North Pole computer center and Googled the word "horses." His computer screen was soon overflowing with information. There was way *too much* information about horses! Next he Googled "happy horse" and up popped a website: happyhorseranchlexingtonmi.com. Alfred quickly typed the address into the Santa-Cam camera and a vision of majestic beauty came into view. Alfred saw five horses racing through the snow, all happily playing a game of *follow the leader*.

Next he clicked onto the *Happy Horse Ranch* information center. Another screen appeared with pictures of five horses. Alfred clicked on the picture of each horse one at a time.

Horse #1: Name: Bobby, Breed: Quarter Horse, Ht: 15/2hh, Wt: 1,050 lbs, Color: Chestnut, Age: 27 yrs. Special Remarks: Injured Rescue Horse-likes carrots. Health restored.

Horse #2: Name: Buddy, Breed: Quarter Horse/Egyptian Arabian, Ht:15hh, Wt: 1,085 lbs, Color: Dark Bay with black mane and tail, Age: 28 yrs, Special Remarks: Abused Rescue Horse-likes peppermint candies.

Horse #3: Name: Cody, Breed: Quarter Horse, Ht:16hh, Wt: 1,300 lbs, Color: Red Dun, Age:13 yrs. Special Remarks: Rescued Racetrack Horse-likes cookies.

Horse #4: Name: Copper, Breed: Arabian, Ht:14/2hh, Wt: 800 lbs, Color: Copper with flaxen mane and tail, Age: 35 yrs: Special Remarks: Neglected–Totally attached to Zip-likes hugs.

Horse #5: Name: Zip, Breed: Percheron/Morgan, Ht: 6hh, Wt. 1,630 lbs, Color: Black, Special Remarks: Abandoned Rescue Horse-Totally attached to Copper- likes all treats.

Alfred asked Santa to come and see what his computer search had revealed. The tiny bell on the tip of his elf hat jingled as he jumped up and down, hardly able to control his excitement. "Santa, these horses look perfect to pull your sleigh full of toys. They are graceful, powerful and extremely happy, and all five were rescue horses. Do you think they may be the ones to *Rescue Christmas?*"

"They look perfect Alfred, but I only see five. We need eight horses to pull my sleigh, since it will be loaded with

presents for all the boys and girls. You can't expect only five horses to take the place of my eight reindeer," Santa sighed.

"Santa, maybe there are more horses inside the barn that we cannot see, but look at the information on Zip, the big black Percheron. He is probably as powerful as two reindeer. There is another named Cody that looks just as big and powerful. Those five horses may be able to pull your sleigh with ease," said Alfred.

"Yes! Yes! There is no time to waste. Take Elf Tabitha with you and go to this *Happy Horse Ranch* and investigate these horses and report back quickly on you Santa satellite phone. I will be waiting for your call. Hurry Alfred! Hurry!"

Alfred and Tabitha rushed to the hangar and climbed aboard the Santa Jet Sled. The shiny red sled blasted down the snowy runway and rocketed into the sky among the twinkling stars, with its GPS system set on Lexington, Michigan, U.S.A.

Chapter 2

*I*t was just past midnight at the *Happy Horse Ranch*. Zip, Copper, Bobby, Buddy and Cody stood in their stalls watching the feathery flakes of snow slowly floating to the moonlit ground. All of a sudden the flakes of snow transformed into a shower of sparkling lights. The horses watched in awe as a small jet sled burst through the lights and circled the pasture of the *Happy Horse Ranch*. Only Zip, the dominant horse of the herd, exited his stall to confront the mystery in the sky. The other horses whinnied nervously from their stalls.

The Santa Jet Sled landed with a thud and skidded across the snowy pasture, coming to a stop behind the barn. Alfred and Tabitha disembarked from the sled and trudged through the deep snow. Suddenly, the ground shook with the thundering of hooves.

Alfred and Tabitha shuddered in fear as a huge black horse materialized through a cloud of snow. Steam vapors shot from his nose as he bent down to confront the intruders. He stomped his huge front hoof inches away from the elves, as they huddled together against the wall of the barn. The ground trembled each time Zip slammed his hoof to the ground. "Quickly Alfred, blow some magic Christmas dust into his nose so he will know that we are friends of Santa," Tabitha whispered. Alfred was fumbling with the bag of Christmas dust when Zip let out a whinny that pierced the air, as he called for the other horses to join him.

Out of nowhere four more horses appeared behind Zip. Their eyes were riveted on the tiny elves. Bobby whinnied and pinned his ears back, threatening Alfred and Tabitha. Copper stood slightly to the rear of his protector Zip and gazed curiously at the elves. Buddy stayed behind Bobby so he could easily flee, if necessary, but Cody pushed his way to the front of the herd and stood next to Zip staring intently at the strange looking knee-high elves. They had pointed ears and large expressive eyes. Both were dressed in green suits with gold buttons that jingled. They wore red velvet

Nordic boots with pointed toes and red elf hats with a tiny gold bell on the tassel.

Cody cautiously bent his neck down, put his nose on Alfred's chest, and gently nudged him. Alfred tumbled backward and fell against Tabitha, who yelled, "Christmas dust Alfred! Hurry! Blow it in his nose! Hurry, hurry, hurry!" Alfred took a deep breath and blew the magic Christmas dust into the air. Millions of tiny sparks lighted the sky surrounding the horses and the entire *Happy Horse Ranch*.

The horses stood motionless after breathing the magic Christmas dust that tickled their nose. Somehow they immediately knew that Alfred and Tabitha were friends, who were indeed sent by Santa Claus. They stood in a circle surrounding Alfred and Tabitha, softly nickering. The magic dust enabled the Elves to understand their *special equine language*. The horses all started talking at the same time.

Zip asked, "Why aren't you at the North Pole helping Santa load his sleigh with toys?"

Bobby reminded the Elves that his Christmas stocking is always filled with carrots and peppermint candy on Christmas Eve. Buddy told the Elves that his Christmas stocking was hanging on his stall door and he also liked peppermint candies and carrots. Copper wanted to know why Santa sent Alfred and Tabitha to the *Happy Horse Ranch* and Cody asked if Mrs. Claus sent any of her special oatmeal cookies.

"Give me a moment and I will answer all of your questions. Let me tell you why Santa sent us here," Alfred said. The horses dropped their heads down low, waiting for Alfred to explain.

"Santa needs you. His reindeer are sick with the reindeer flu and will not be well in time to pull his sleigh full of toys on Christmas Eve for the boys and girls of the world. You must be the ones to replace Santa's reindeer and *Rescue Christmas.*"

Whinnies of joy pierced the frosty air as the horses pranced with excitement.

Cody asked, "Will the children leave cookies and carrots out for us on Christmas Eve?"

"I've never pulled a sleigh before," said Bobby.

"Will I be next to Zip," Copper wanted to know.

"Are you going to ask our dad if we can go," asked Buddy?

"Horses can't fly," Zip added.

Alfred smiled broadly through his short gray beard and raised his hand motioning for silence. The horses stood quietly with their ears pointing forward, so they could listen intently to what Alfred had to say.

"Each of you understands what it is like to be rescued. Now you will be able to rescue the happiest time of the year, *Christmas.* Yes Cody, the children leave cookies and carrots for you to enjoy. Bobby, do not be concerned, you will be able to pull Santa's sleigh with ease. Copper, fear not, you will be close to Zip. Buddy, I have a note written by Santa to leave on the barn door for your dad explaining how you are rescuing Christmas. And finally

Zip, horses can fly when sprinkled with magic flying powder. We may have to put a few extra sprinkles on you, but you will be able to fly. There is one more thing that you need to know. The magic flying powder will only allow you to fly until daybreak on Christmas Day."

"Tabitha, do you have something that you would like to say?"

"Merry Christmas! It's going to be Equine time at Christmas time," Tabitha shouted, as she jumped up and down with glee. The horses reared up on their hind legs, whinnied with joy, and raced across the snowy pastures, creating whirlwinds of snow. The horses from the *Happy Horse Ranch* were ready to learn how to fly so they could rescue Christmas.

Chapter 3

Santa stood next to his sleigh full of toys at the North Pole waiting to welcome the horses from *the Happy Horse Ranch*. "I wonder if they will soar through the sky with the beauty and grace of my reindeer they replace. There are only five instead of eight. I hope my toys will not be delivered late." Santa looked into his Santa-Cam and watched Alfred and Tabitha line up the horses single file in the snow-covered pasture. He could see the excitement in the horses, as they patiently waited their turn to be sprinkled with magic flying powder. Santa looked closely at Zip and wondered if there would be enough magic flying powder left to lift such a big horse off the ground.

Santa stared intently into the Santa-Cam, as Alfred and Tabitha placed the horses in the positions that they would be harnessed to Santa's sleigh on Christmas Eve. He called out to Mrs. Claus and all of his elves, "Come here and watch! The horses are about to be sprinkled with my magic flying powder." The excitement mounted. Mrs. Claus hugged Santa tightly and the elves cheered for the horses, knowing that they were the only hope to rescue Christmas. They stared into the Santa-Cam and waited to see if the magic flying powder would lift the horses from the pasture of the *Happy Horse Ranch.*

The powerful Zip was placed in the number one spot, followed by Copper and Buddy, who were side by side behind him, then Cody and Bobby together, bringing up the rear of the line.

Alfred looked up at Zip and said, "When I sprinkle you with Santa's magic flying powder you must gallop across the pasture and jump into the air. Keep your head pointed high and you will soar through the sky. When you return to the ground, point your head down. You must be in the air before you come to the fence at the far end of the pasture."

Zip whinnied his understanding of Alfred's instructions. He peered across the pasture that was aglow in moonlight. Snow drifts hugged the wooden fence that circled the pasture. He stomped his huge feet and let out a neigh. He was ready to fly.

Tabitha sprinkled the magic flying powder on Zip's legs and hooves. "Go Zip! Fly into the sky!" Alfred shouted. Whinnies of encouragement burst through the air. The ground shook as Zip galloped at full speed across the snow covered pasture. The fence at the end of the pasture was fast approaching. Tabitha and Alfred held their breath. Zip jumped into the air, but could not get high enough to fly over the fence. At the last second he pointed his head down and crashed to the ground, landing in the deep snow bank at the end of the pasture. He came trotting back covered in snow. "I don't think I will be able to fly and help rescue Christmas. I am just too big to get off the ground," Zip said disappointedly.

"Yes you can," snorted Bobby.

"You can do it Zip," whinnied Buddy.

"Please Zip, you can't let the children down," nickered Copper.

"You must lead the way Zip."

"We must rescue Christmas," said Cody.

Alfred's Santa phone beeped and an instant message from Santa appeared on the screen. "Tell Zip not to be discouraged. I know what must be done. He must be sprinkled from head to hoof with magic flying powder. Do not fear. He will soar like my reindeer."

Alfred read Santa's message to the horses. Zip tossed his head back and let out a huge whinny of happiness. "I am ready to try again and this time I will fly through the sky," he said. Cheers and whinnies rocketed toward the stars, as the horses danced with merriment.

Alfred asked Cody to come forward and stand next to Zip. "Cody, bend your head down so Tabitha can climb on your neck and then lift you onto Zip's back." Cody nodded and bent his head down low to the ground.

"Climb up Tabitha and sprinkle extra magic flying powder on Zip so he is covered from head to hoof." Tabitha grabbed Cody's mane and was lifted high into the air. She stepped onto Zip's back with two bags of magic flying powder.

"How do I get down after I sprinkle him with magic flying powder," she asked?

"Step back quickly onto Cody and he will lower you to the ground," Alfred yelled up to her.

Tabitha shook the bag of sprinkles onto Zip's tail and back. Zip whinnied with excitement as the sprinkles floated down on his hind legs and hooves. She then opened the second bag and sprinkled Zip's flowing mane. Zip pawed the ground nervously. "Hurry Tabitha, sprinkle my head. I can feel that I am almost ready to fly high in the sky." She sprinkled the remaining magic flying powder onto his neck and head. Zip's muscular body shook with energy. He tossed his head skyward, as he breathed in the last few sprinkles of the magic flying powder.

"Hang on Tabitha. I can't wait. I must fly." The ground quaked as Zip galloped across the snowy pasture with Tabitha clinging to his mane. Her large blue eyes widened and her blonde ponytail bounced up and down with the rhythm of the pounding hooves. "Whoa! Stop! Help! Get me down!" she screamed. The horses cheered, as Zip lifted his head and soared over the wooden fence into the moonlit sky. Tabitha's words could faintly

be heard drifting down on flakes of snow from high in the sky. "I will be brave. Christmas we must save."

Chapter 4

Zip and Tabitha zoomed through the night guided by the bright stars. They flew along the shoreline of Lake Huron into the sleepy Village of Lexington. Christmas lights twinkled on the houses and stores. The old Victorian streetlamp posts were decorated with red and white candy canes and wrapped in festive garland. The streets were empty except for a single police car that cruised slowly down Main Street. Zip lowered his head and glided above the police car. He whinnied with joy and then flew high into the sky. Tabitha yelled, "Merry Christmas!" as they disappeared from sight. The police officer rubbed his eyes and stared in disbelief. He called the police dispatch center to report that he had just witnessed an Unidentified Flying Object heading north from Lexington.

Zip and Tabitha flew back to the *Happy Horse Ranch*, eager to help get the other horses into the sky. "Hang onto my mane tightly, Tabitha. I am dropping my head down to get closer to the ground. I want my barn buddies to look up and see us skimming above the tree tops."

Zip circled over the woods surrounding the pasture and released an enormous whinny that bounced from tree to tree. The night became alive from the cheering voices of the wild animals that lived in the woods surrounding the *Happy Horse Ranch*. Bobby, Buddy, Cody and Copper answered Zip with ear piercing whinnies of their own. Alfred yelled, "Go Zip, go!"

"Let's land back in the pasture now Zip. The other horses must also be able to practice flying so we can head to the North Pole and join Santa Claus," said Tabitha, as they swooped above the roof of the barn.

"Look out below. We are coming in for a landing," Zip whinnied. Then there was a big *thud* as Zip and Tabitha landed in an explosion of snow. "Wow Zip, I think that we are going to work on your landing skills. It was kind of a rough landing. Remember, when you land on the rooftops of all the homes it must be done gently."

"I'm sorry Tabitha. I must have had my head held too low. I will know what to do next time. Did I do okay, other than the rough landing?"

"Santa will be proud to have you lead the horses of the *Happy Horse Ranch* around the world with toys for all the children," Tabitha said triumphantly. Zip bucked with sheer joy. Tabitha was tossed into the air and landed in a deep snow bank. Alfred and the horses laughed, as Tabitha's head popped out of the snow wearing a big smile. "Let's get all the horses into the air," she gleefully shouted.

Buddy and Copper lined up side by side, waiting to take their turn. Buddy pawed the ground nervously, as vapors of steam shot from his nostrils. Copper stood next to him, trembling with fear. "I can't fly without Zip," he stammered.

"If Zip can fly, so can we. Be confident my little friend. I will be by your side," said Buddy.

Zip trotted up to Copper and they touched noses. Zip whispered into Copper's ear, filling him with confidence. "Sprinkle us with the magic

flying powder, Tabitha. Buddy and I are ready to fly behind the hips of mighty Zip and help rescue Christmas for the children of the world," Copper snorted.

Tabitha removed two bags of magic flying powder from the Jet Sled and hurried back to the two horses. Buddy nervously snorted puffs of steam from his nose. Copper raised his head and whinnied loudly. Cody again lifted the tiny elves with their magic flying powder into the air, placing them on Buddy and Copper's backs. "Do not fear my friends. High above the ground you will be, with every moment filled with glee," Alfred shouted.

The elves scampered from head to tail, sprinkling the magic flying powder on Buddy and Copper. There was a sudden burst of energy and the air was filled with blinding snow. Alfred and Tabitha were somersaulted to the ground amid the clashing of hooves. When the air cleared the elves watched in awe, as Buddy and Copper flew high above the *Happy Horse Ranch.*

Buddy and Copper were indeed filled with glee, as Alfred had promised they would be. Mighty Zip zoomed back into the sky so he would be close to his little buddy, Copper. He whinnied to Bobby and Cody far below. "Get into the air. To the North Pole we must go!"

Now it was time for Bobby and Cody to join their friends. They were quickly sprinkled with magic flying powder by the elves. There was the sound of clashing hooves and cheers from Tabitha and Alfred that ricocheted across the land, as Bobby and Cody zoomed into the sky. The happy whinnies from the horses were carried through the atmosphere on soft moonbeams. It was almost time to *rescue Christmas.*

Santa and Mrs. Claus watched the horses on the Santa-Cam soaring through the sky, all illuminated by the light of the moon and the sparkling stars. It was such a beautiful sight to watch the horses, for indeed they had all of the beauty and grace of the reindeer.

"These are the horses that will *rescue Christmas*," declared Santa. The Arctic Circle quaked with screams of revelry. The elves danced around the sled that was full of toys that were waiting to be delivered by Santa on Christmas Eve. The horses from the *Happy Horse Ranch* in Lexington, Michigan, U.S.A. would soon be on their way to the North Pole.

The horses landed back in the pasture of the *Happy Horse Ranch*, amid a few thuds, bumps and skids to receive final instructions for their fight to the North Pole.

Chapter 5

The *Happy Horse Ranch* was alive with excitement. "Each of you did great on your maiden flight. Now, I want you to line up just like you will when you pull Santa's sleigh full of toys. Zip, you will be first. Buddy and Copper, stand side by side behind Zip. Bobby and Cody, get behind Buddy and Copper," said Alfred.

"Are you going to tell to our dad where we are," asked Buddy?

Alfred pulled an envelope from his coat pocket and held it up. "This is the note from Santa to your dad. I will read it to you and leave it on the barn door." Alfred put on a pair of wire-frame spectacles. He read Santa's note to the horses.

To the Dad of the horses of the Happy Horse Ranch:

I had to ask your horses to save Christmas. My reindeer have the flu and are unable to pull my sleigh full of toys for the boys and girls around the world. Your powerful and graceful horses are the only hope to deliver my toys on Christmas Eve.

They have been sprinkled with magic flying powder, which allows them to fly. They will be returned by daylight on Christmas Day.

Thank you from all the boys and girls of the world.

Merry Christmas,

Santa Claus

"We can't leave without Jaboozala," said Cody. The other horses nickered in agreement.

"We must take her with us. She will be lonely and afraid if we are gone. We protect her. She can't spend Christmas Eve by herself," said Buddy.

"Who is Jaboozala? Is she another horse inside the barn," asked Tabitha?

"Follow us," Zip answered, as the horses trotted to the barn. The horses started softly nickering to let Jaboozala know that it was safe to come out of the barn. Alfred and Tabitha watched the barn intently, wondering *who* or *what* was Jaboozala.

A shorthair black cat with a spattering of orange spots and large green eyes peeked out from a horse stall. Jaboozala darted from the barn and stood next to Buddy. She looked at the Elves and meowed.

"I will have to get Santa's permission," said Alfred. The words were barely out of Alfred's mouth when the Santa-Cam jingled, and Santa appeared on the screen. "Ho! Ho! Ho! Bring Jaboozala with you, Alfred. She can ride in my sleigh next to me on Christmas Eve."

The elves walked between the horses legs and patted Jaboozala on her head. There were purrs of contentment from Jaboozala and whinnies of joy from the horses.

Alfred took the note from Santa and added a post script. "Jaboozala is also with the horses."

He then positioned the horses in take-off position to depart for the North Pole. Alfred gave final take-off instructions to the horses.

"Tabitha, you must ride on Zip's back so there is room in the Jet Sled for Jaboozala. You must all gallop as one across the pasture. Tabitha will count to five, and then you must lift your head up to the sky. When you are in the air, circle above the barn until Jaboozala and I join you."

"Can't Jaboozala ride on Zip's back?" Tabitha asked. "No, her claws will dig into me," Zip responded. "You will be fine Tabitha," assured Alfred. Cody lowered his head, and Tabitha climbed up his neck. She was lowered onto Zip's back.

"Don't forget to count to five, Tabitha. Get ready! Get set! GO!" The horses were a picture of grace and beauty, as they galloped across the pasture. Tabitha counted quickly, as she watched the fence at the far end of the pasture fast approach. "One, two, three, four, *five!*" she screamed. The horses raised their heads up and were lifted into the night sky.

Alfred cheered as Tabitha and the horses circled overhead. They were ready to replace Santa's reindeer.

Alfred got a small bag of magic Christmas dust from the Jet Sled and rubbed some into Jaboozala's fur. She instantly knew that she would be safe flying to the North Pole in Santa's sled, which suddenly came alive in a burst of flames shot from the exhaust. "Here we go, Jaboozala. We are on our way to *rescue Christmas.*"

The little jet sled streaked into the sky and circled the *Happy Horse Ranch*. Alfred and Jaboozala hovered in front of Zip and Tabitha. "Okay, let's go and rescue Christmas." The exuberant whinnies and joyful shouts drifted over the now-empty landscape of the *Happy Horse Ranch*.

Chapter 6

*S*adness prevailed in countries around the globe, as news flooded the airways that Santa's reindeer were sick with the reindeer flu. They would not be able to pull Santa's sleigh full of toys to the boys and girls of the world. The international news networks broadcast Santa's dilemma to a dejected world population. Santa's desperate situation flashed across the Internet, Facebook and Twitter at the speed of light. There would be no *clitter clatter* of reindeer hooves on rooftops. Newspaper headlines screamed: *"NO SANTA CLAUS THIS YEAR!"* World prayers drifted to the heavens requesting *divine intervention* to help Santa find a way to deliver his toys. Little did the world know that Santa was working on a plan to rescue Christmas. His elves, Alfred and Tabitha had already been hard at work at the *Happy Horse Ranch* in Lexington, Michigan, U.S.A.

Dawn broke at the home of Mr. and Mrs. Holly as the first rays of sunshine peeked through the windows, blending the sun's warmth with the aroma of freshly brewed coffee. The Hollys always enjoyed a steaming cup of coffee together before Mr. Holly went to the barn to take care of his beloved horses. He was dad to the horses at the *Happy Horse Ranch*.

When he finished his beverage, he headed to the barn with bags of carrots and peppermint candies to put in the horses Christmas stockings that were hanging on their stall doors. He also brought a can of tuna for Jaboozala's stocking. "It will be so much fun to fill the stockings with special treats and then watch the joy and happiness on Christmas morning," he thought to himself.

Snowflakes tickled his nose in the crisp early morning air. He hummed his favorite song, "*Here comes Santa Claus,*" as he approached the barn. *It was such a joyful time of year.* He called to his horses that were always standing by the fence waiting to greet him. But alas, there were no horses to be seen. "Bobby, Buddy, Cody, Copper, Zip...Where are you?" But the pasture was silent. There was no thunderings of hooves coming to greet him. There weren't the usual greetings of whinnies and nickers. *SOMETHING WAS WRONG!*

Mr. Holly felt his chest begin to tighten with fear. He opened the gate and ran into the pasture. He scanned his ten acres, looking for any sign of the horses. But the pasture was empty except for their hoof prints and tracks from a small sled in the fresh fallen snow.

The hoof prints were grouped on top of the small rise next to the barn. The biggest ones belonged to Zip. The other four horses were lined up in pairs behind him. The hoof prints headed due west toward the back fence line.

Mr. Holly found chunks of snow with hoof designs. He knew that the horses had to be galloping fast to kick out snow hardened hoof prints. He followed the tracks to the west pasture fence line. All five sets of prints mysteriously disappeared at the end of the pasture. The fence had not been knocked down and there were no signs of any horses on the other side.

"How can this be? Horses can't fly. They can't disappear into thin air!" he exclaimed.

He hurried to the barn to see if the horses might be in their stalls. There was a red envelope taped to the barn door addressed to "Mr. Holly, Happy Horse Ranch, Lexington, Michigan" with a return address of "Santa Claus, North Pole."

He stared at the envelope in disbelief. His hands trembled as he removed Santa's note amid a burst of sparkling glitter that filled the air. Suddenly he was filled with joy and happiness from the magic of Santa, as he read the note:

To the Dad of the horses of the Happy Horse Ranch:

I had to ask your horses to save Christmas. My reindeer have the flu and are unable to pull my sleigh full of toys for the boys and girls around the world. Your powerful and graceful horses are the only hope to deliver my toys on Christmas Eve.

"They have been sprinkled with magic flying powder, which allows them to fly. They will be returned by daylight on Christmas day.

Thank you from all the boys and girls of the world.

Merry Christmas,

Santa Claus

P.S. Jaboozala is also with us.

Elf Alfred

Mr. Holly hurried to tell his wife the thrilling news that Bobby, Buddy, Cody, Copper and Zip were on their way to the North Pole to pull Santa's sleigh filled with toys for the children of the world.

Mrs. Holly was standing on the porch frantically waving her arms. "A news bulletin just came on TV. Santa just sent an e-mail to the news outlets around the world. He has found replacements for his flu stricken reindeer. Santa's sleigh is going to be pulled by five powerful and graceful horses," she yelled excitedly.

"I know! I know! I have a note from Santa. It's *our* horses that are going to *rescue Christmas.* They are gone! They are on their way to Santa's Village at the North Pole. Jaboozala even went with them! Read this note…our horses are going to *rescue* Christmas."

Mrs. Holly read Santa's note. Tears of happiness trickled down her cheeks. Santa had indeed chosen horses of strength, courage, beauty and grace. "Santa's toys won't be delivered late. He will be in stride with our horse's gait," she laughed.

The Hollys gave each other a big hug. They were filled with pride, as they looked out the window at the empty snow-covered pastures. They smiled as they watched the hoof prints and the tracks of a tiny sled disappear beneath a blanket of freshly-falling snow.

Santa's e-mail dominated the world news:

To: All world news information outlets.

From: SantaClausNorthPole.org

Subject: Christmas Rescue

Be advised that my flu stricken reindeer are still ill. I am replacing them with five powerful, graceful and happy horses from a rescue ranch in the Village of Lexington, State of Michigan, U.S.A. They have been sprinkled with magic flying powder and are presently on their way to the North Pole, accompanied by my elves Tabitha and Alfred.

Will the horses be able to replace my reindeer? You must *believe* in the *magic of Christmas.*

Santa

Chapter 7

*T*he shiny red Jet Sled headed north along the frozen shoreline of Lake Huron with the horses from the *Happy Horse* Ranch gliding behind in the warm jetstream. They soon approached the Straits of Mackinaw, where Lake Michigan and Lake Huron mixed their icy blue waters. Flying high over the Mackinaw Bridge, the tiny sled and horses crossed into the heavily forested Upper Peninsula of Michigan.

The horses nickered back and forth to each other as they soared above the snow-covered blacken forests. "I sure hope we don't run out of magic flying powder." "There are black bears and grey wolves roaming through the trees below." "When are we going to be there, Tabitha?"

"Don't be afraid my friends. Enjoy the magic of flight. Alfred will be increasing our speed once you are accustomed to flying. Look at me on the back of Zip. I am not afraid. " See that bright star high in the sky? That is the North Star, Polaris. It is directly above Santa's Village at the North Pole. You will soon be at the happiest place on earth," she said.

As they approached the border between the United States and Canada, Alfred signaled an increase in speed. The small group rocketed across the Province of Ontario, Hudson Bay, the Gulf of Boothia and the Northwest Territories. The forests slowly disappeared. Mountains of snow and ice rose upward. Polaris shined its might, lighting the way to Santa's Village.

Shortly after crossing the North Magnetic Pole the dancing lights of Santa's Village lighted the sky. Children Christmas songs rose above the village, serenading the millions of bright stars hovering high above. The flashing red and green runway lights guided the tiny Jet Sled and horses down for a landing.

"Remember, slowly lower your heads down for a smooth landing," shouted Tabitha.

Alfred guided the Jet Sled between the landing lights onto the runway and touched down in a feathery cloud of snow.

Tabitha and Zip, Buddy and Copper, Bobby and Cody landed smoothly, but at a full gallop. "Whoa, slow down, "Tabitha yelled. The horses slowed to a gentle walk through the dancing snowflakes. Welcoming cheers, dancing elves and Christmas music erupted throughout Santa's Village as the horses approached the welcoming crowd. They all sensed a feeling of well being, joy, and especially happiness.

Standing in front of the cheering crowd was Santa himself. His bright red Santa suit had furry white trim on the sleeves and a strip running from his neck to the top of a wide black belt. The belt had a large gold buckle. Inscribed on the buckle was the word *Believe.* His red trousers adorned with white fur trim were tucked into his shiny black boots. He wore white gloves and a red tassel cap with a white ball on the end.

Santa's stood over six feet tall and weighed a few chocolate chip cookies in excess of two hundred pounds. A pair of clear glasses sat just below the bridge of his nose. He had rosy red cheeks and a long white beard that sat on his slightly rounded belly. Santa's soft eyes twinkled and his flowing white beard jiggled on his chest when he said, "Ho! Ho! Ho! Welcome my friends. Thank you on behalf of all the boys and girls of the world for *rescuing Christmas.*"

The elves shouted with delight and Tabitha slid down Zip's neck to join in the celebration. Santa picked up Jaboozala and placed her on his shoulder. She let out a loud meow and started purring. The horses whinnied and reared up on their hind legs. Then the song, *Here Comes Santa Claus* played loudly throughout Santa's Village.

Santa picked up an orange sack, inscribed with the word *Carrots.* He walked over to the horses. He pulled two carrots out and stood in front of Zip. "Here, my mighty friends, is a treat for you." He gave each horse two carrots and a big hug. Each horse nickered and rubbed Santa's rosy cheek with their soft noses.

All of a sudden there was a loud *"ACHOO!"* Bobby's nose had been tickled by Santa's beard, and he sneezed bits of carrot all over Santa! Santa's glasses frosted over from the warm blast of moist air. His snowy white beard was filled with flecks of orange carrot bits. There was a deafening silence for a moment, and then Santa burst into booming laughter as he hugged Bobby around his neck. Bobby placed his head on Santa's shoulder and tried licking the flecks of carrot from his beard. The elves rolled on the ground in laughter and the horses whinnied with excitement.

"Ho! Ho! Ho! Follow me my friends. You are going to get a tour of my village," said Santa. He reached down, picked up Jaboozala, patted her gently on her head, placed her on his shoulder and whispered, "Do not be afraid, Jaboozala." She snuggled on Santa's neck and purred softly.

Zip uttered a gentle nicker toward Santa and dropped his head to the ground. Santa turned and said, "What is it Zip? Is something wrong?"

"He is offering you a ride, Santa," giggled Tabitha. Zip nodded his head up and down and let out a deep whinny of agreement.

"Thank you my friend. It will be an honor to ride into my village on your strong back." Santa stood next to Zip's side and looked up. The elves broke into giggles and the horses nickered at Santa's dilemma. Zip snorted with glee and dropped down on his knees. "Thank you, Zip," said Santa, as he climbed on his back, and Zip lifted Santa high above the dancing elves.

'Wait!" said Alfred. "Come on Tabitha." The two elves stood by Cody's knee, looked up and smiled. Cody neighed and dropped his head. Alfred and Tabitha quickly scampered up his neck and onto his back. "Now we are ready, Santa."

The jolly procession, with Santa straddling Zip, trotted triumphantly into Santa's Village. Yes indeed, these were the horses that were going to *rescue Christmas*.

Chapter 8

*S*anta's e-mail created excitement and hope across the world. Stories of Santa's attempt to *rescue Christmas crackled* across all communication networks. Many news headlines, from across the country, offered hope. A few cast doubt if horses would be able to *rescue Christmas*.

"LEXINGTON HORSES TO THE RESCUE" (*The Detroit Tribune*)

HORSES FROM LEXINGTON, MICHIGAN ARE SANTA'S LAST CHANCE!" (*The Texas Union Free Press*)

"SANTA'S AILING REINDEER REPLACED WITH RESCUE HORSES!" (*The Alaska News*)

"CAN HORSES REALLY RESCUE CHRISTMAS?" (*The Massachusetts Minuteman*)

SANTA SAYS, "BELIEVE!"
(*The North Pole Village News*)

"THEY CAN DO IT!"
(*The Lexington Gazette*)

An avalanche of reporters, news teams and well wishers descended upon the *Happy Horse Ranch*. Mr. and Mrs. Jolly stood on their front porch and stared in awe at the sights and sounds. There were news trucks with satellite dishes, camera crews shooting live video, honking horns, children yelling, banners waving and a news helicopter circling overhead.

The dark blue Lexington police chief's squad car snaked through the cars, trucks and the mass of well wishers that jammed the narrow snow-covered country road and pulled into the driveway of the *Happy Horse Ranch*.

The village mayor stepped from the vehicle and waved to the applauding crowd. The public address system on the roof of the police car crackled and the police chief's voice asked for quiet. The crowd quieted and the mayor spoke into the microphone.

"Merry Christmas and welcome to Lexington and the Happy Horse Ranch." The crowd erupted with cheering and shouts of joy. She continued, "Margaret and Dan Holly have agreed to tell you about their five horses that have been asked by Santa to *rescue Christmas.*"

Mr. and Mrs. Holly stood on their porch under blinking red and blue Christmas lights that decorated their house. The porch spindles and rails were wrapped in red and white garland. Frosty the Snowman sat on the porch with his eyes of black coal peeking beneath his stove pipe hat. His carrot nose had long since been sacrificed for a horse treat. The smell of fresh baked cookies drifted down the steps into the crowd.

The Hollys had broad smiles on their faces and beamed with pride. Shouts came from the crowd. "Are your horses at the North Pole? Can they take the place of eight reindeer? When did you find out they were gone? Can we go in the barn? Is it true that your barn cat went with them? Did you hear them leave? Did you talk to Santa? Will the Christmas presents be delivered to the boys and girls?"

Then a melodious chant of, "Go Zip go! Go Zip go! Go Zip go!" echoed through the crowd. Then more cheers rang out. "Hooray for Bobby, Buddy, Copper and Cody! Hooray for Bobby, Buddy, Copper and Cody!"

Mr. Holly wore a red and black plaid wool coat that covered his broad chest and tall frame. His sheepskin boots, blue jeans and rawhide gloves accented his rugged good looks. Piercing blue eyes twinkled beneath the brim of a western hat and his neatly trimmed mustache was color coordinated with his salt and pepper hair. He had a smile that radiated warmth, caring and strength. He raised his arms and signaled *thumbs up* to everyone and shouted, "Merry Christmas!"

Mrs. Holly stood next to her husband, squeezing his arm and jumping up and down with excitement. Her warm features were slightly hidden by the parka of the forest green winter coat that surrounded her face. A red Santa scarf bearing a picture of Santa circled her neck. The word *Believe* was embroidered beneath his picture. Her long auburn hair peeked out from the parka. Warmth radiated from her dark sparkling eyes and her welcoming smile. She threw her arms above her head and hollered to the crowd, "Go Zip go! Go Zip go!" Everyone joined in and the *Happy Horse Ranch* rocked to the rhythmical beat of "Go Zip go! Go Zip go!"

The police chief again asked for quiet, so Mr. Holly could speak. The crowd waited to hear the story of how the horses from *the Happy Horse Ranch* were going to rescue Christmas.

"My friends, I am going to read to you the note that was left on my barn door on the morning of December 23. It reads as follows;

"To the dad of the horses of the Happy Horse Ranch:

I had to ask your horses to save Christmas. My reindeer have the flu and are unable to pull my sleigh full of toys for the boys and girls around the world. Your powerful and graceful horses are the only hope to deliver my toys on Christmas Eve.

They have been sprinkled with magic flying powder, which allows them to fly. They will be returned by daylight on Christmas day.

Thank you from all the boys and girls of the world."

Merry Christmas,

Santa Claus

P.S. Jaboozala is also with us.

Elf Alfred

Mr. Holly explained how he discovered the four sets of hoof prints and tiny sleigh marks in the snow ending at the pasture's west fence line. "This is truly a miracle! Bobby, Buddy, Cody, Copper and Zip are going to pull Santa's sleigh full of toys on Christmas Eve and *rescue Christmas!*" he shouted.

Messages of hope posted on Facebook and Twitter crisscrossed the world. Pictures of the cheering crowd dominated the news. Now it was up to the rescue horses of the *Happy Horse Ranch* to rescue Christmas.

Chapter 9

The first stop in Santa's Village was at a large red barn with a green roof surrounded by a red and white candy stripe fence. The roof was long and flat and was lined with blinking lighted Christmas trees running the length of the roof on both sides. "It looks like a rooftop runway," Buddy nickered.

"It is Buddy. I have the extra runway in case of an emergency. The heat from the barn melts the snow on the roof so my reindeer always have a safe landing. This is only for my experienced reindeer. Sometimes the main runway may be under construction or the snow may be very deep and would prevent a safe landing," said Santa.

Santa and Jaboozala slid down from Zip's back. Cody lowered his head, sending Alfred and Tabitha sliding down his neck. They landed on the ground with the sound of two small thuds. There were snickers and nickers, as Alfred and Tabitha dusted off the snow.

"This, my friends, is our reindeer barn; the home of Dasher, Dancer, Vixen, Comet, Cupid, Donner, Blitzen and of course, Rudolph. As you know, all of my reindeer have the reindeer flu, but it is not contagious to horses. They are fast asleep in their stalls," said Santa.

He pushed a round green button on the fencepost and the large barn doors slid open. The walls of the barn were lined with large box stalls, each decorated with candy canes and shiny garland. A sign with the name of each reindeer hung above their stall door. Several inches of sparkling red and green confetti bedding covered the stall floors. Above the stalls was a hayloft filled with green alfalfa hay. The horses walked slowly on the cedar plank floor, peeking into the stalls and eyeing the green hay stacked above. Jaboozala hopped from Santa's shoulder into the hayloft.

"I am going to play in the hay," meowed Jaboozala.

"Have fun and be sure to take a long cat nap. We have a long sleigh ride tonight, Jaboozala," said Santa. She watched Santa, Tabitha, Alfred and the horses continue down the aisle way. She gave a contented meow and went exploring in the hayloft.

"The reindeer are larger than I thought," said Bobby.

"Yes, they are very muscular and have very big antlers," Cody added.

"Blitzen is as big as you, Copper," Buddy nickered.

"You're right, Buddy, but I am better looking. Blitzen doesn't have a beautiful flaxen mane and tail. He doesn't have my beautiful copper color or large brown eyes, like I do."

"I agree, Copper. But he is still beautiful. Let's go see what Zip and Santa are doing."

Santa and Zip were standing by the end stall that had a sign with the name *Rudolph* above the door. Alfred, Tabitha, Bobby. Buddy and Copper hurried to join them. There in the stall was *Rudolph the Red Nose Reindeer!* He was lying down with his front feet tucked underneath his brawny chest. His large brown eyes slowly opened and then closed again.

His nose cast a dim red glow. His head, weighed down by a large set of shiny antlers, rested in the glittering bedding in his stall.

Standing next to Rudolph was a small elf, who was wearing a white physician jacket. He held a small stethoscope on Rudolph's chest and listened intently. He removed the stethoscope from his large pointed elf ears, fumbled through his medical bag and a removed a bottle that read, *Reindeer Flu Syrup.* He whispered something in Rudolph's ear. Rudolph stirred, raised his head and opened his mouth. Dr. Sweitzer, the Chief of Veterinary Medicine, squeezed the contents of the small bottle into his mouth. Rudolph murmured several low grunts and his nose flickered brightly for a moment, only to return to a dim glow.

Doctor Sweitzer peered over his wire frame glasses at Santa and said, "Do not worry, Santa. Rudolph is getting stronger each day. All of the reindeer will soon be better. However, they will not recover in time to pull your sleigh full of toys on Christmas Eve."

Santa sighed, smiled broadly, and said, " These five powerful and happy horses will pull my sleigh full of toys, Dr. Sweitzer."

Dr. Sweitzer nodded his head in agreement and said, "Zip, come into the stall and lower your head next to Rudolph. He wants to talk with you." Zip hesitated and looked at Santa for reassurance. Santa smiled and nodded his head.

Zip stepped gingerly into Rudolph's stall and cautiously lowered his head next to Rudolph's shiny pointed antlers. Rudolph opened his eyes and uttered a few low reindeer grunts into Zip's ear. Zip nodded his head up and down responding with low sounding nickers.

Then it happened! **Rudolph slowly lifted his head and touched noses with Zip!**

Crimson bolts of lightning streaked skyward. Zip jumped up and reared into the air on his hind legs and let out a piercing whinny that shook the buildings in Santa's Village. Dr. Sweitzer hid behind Rudolph. Santa, Tabitha and Alfred ducked behind Bobby, Buddy, and Copper, as Zip's mighty front hooves crashed to the ground lighting the air with green and red sparkles. Everyone stared in awe! Zip now had a shiny red nose that glowed very bright. "Santa, he said, I am ready to guide your sleigh tonight."

The elves cheered, the horses whinnied and Santa gave Zip a big hug around the neck. Santa then hugged Rudolph for giving Zip the power to illuminate the night sky. Rudolph made a joyful grunt knowing that there was a mighty horse that would keep Santa on course. Rudolph had no fear. He knew that he would lead Santa's reindeer next year.

The horses crowded around Zip, curious to inspect his new red nose. Buddy asked, "Is your nose hot, Zip?" Bobby said, "You sure look funny." "I am glad that your nose will light up the night, so Santa will have a safe flight," Copper added. Zip whinnied and touched noses with the horses.

"I didn't hear from you Cody. "What do you think of my red nose?" asked Zip There was no answer. The horses turned and looked behind them, but Cody was not there. "Where is Cody," shouted the horses. They looked at Santa for an answer. "I don't know where he is. I thought he was with us," said Santa. "Quickly, we must search the barn."

Tabitha, Alfred and the horses followed Santa down the aisle next to the reindeer stalls. Santa stopped in front of Dasher's stall and looked down at the remnants of green alfalfa lying on the floor. Everyone looked up at the hayloft above the stall. There was a bale of hay minus a few mouthfuls. Cody had stood on his hind legs and munched on the alfalfa, as Dasher slept through it all.

"He must be hungry," laughed Santa. "Would the rest of you like to eat?" There were nickers of excitement from the four horses. "Zip, would you please get a bale of hay down from the loft?" Zip nodded his head in the affirmative and reared up on his hind legs, resting his from legs on the hayloft floor above Dasher's stall.   He grabbed the partially-sampled hay bale with one mighty bite. The green bale of alfalfa had a red glow from Zip's nose, as it tumbled to the floor.

"Eat hardy, my friends. When you are finished we must find Cody. We must fit you with a harness and practice take off and landings with my sleigh full of toys. There is much to do and very little time." The horses quickly devoured the rich tasting alfalfa.

"He may have gone into my village to explore," said Santa. They hurried outside and stood amid the wet flakes of snow accumulating on Santa's Village. "There are his hoof prints," said Tabitha, pointing to a set of partially snow-filled tracks. The snow was rapidly covering Cody's trail, as he headed into Santa's Village.

"Tabitha, take Zip, Copper, Buddy and Bobby back in the barn to the Harness Shop. Elf Henry and his harness makers are waiting to take measurements and start construction. Ask Henry to also make one for Cody, not quite as big as the one for Zip."

"Yes Santa."

"Come with me, my friends. You are each going to have a beautiful harness made especially for you. On Christmas Eve you will *harness the magic of Christmas.*"

"Are you sure you don't need our help in finding Cody," asked Zip?

"Not right now, Zip. We need to have your harnesses made. Time is short. If Alfred and I do not find him quickly we will be back to get you, after your harness measurements."

They followed Tabitha back inside the reindeer barn accompanied by sounds of nickers and clip-clops.

Santa and Alfred stood side by side staring at the large clock that stood in the center of the village square. The clock's tower was constructed of huge blocks of ice that rose high in the snowy sky. At the top sat the clock that had a red face and was twenty-five feet in diameter. The green hour hand was twelve feet long and the minute hand was fourteen feet in length. Inside the bell tower was a gigantic bell that weighed ten tons. The bell gonged six times. "Alfred, we only have fifteen hours before I must leave to deliver toys to the children of the world. I must be in the sky by 9 p.m., so we must hurry."

"We can do it Santa. Let's find Cody and practice a few take offs and landings."

"Yes, we must find Cody. Without his extra strength I won't be able to deliver my toys. Without Cody, there will be no *rescue of Christmas.*"

Chapter 10

Newspapers around the world printed their final Christmas Eve edition with headlines that reflected doubt that Christmas would be rescued.

¿Los caballos pueden rescatar a Navidad? – (Mexico)

圣诞老人之麻烦 ！– (China)

Elfo report, Cody è mancante! – (Italy)

Лошадей можно заменить оленей? – (Russia)

Sie können ausführen es, Santa – (Germany)

סנטה מסייע שמח סוסים חוות – (Israel)

Tro på Santa – (Sweeden)

Nie załamuj się! Santa będzie się w powietrzu! – (Poland)

Bid voor Santa! – (Netherlands)

Cody Missing! Toy delivery in doubt! – (North Pole)

Reporters flocked to the *Happy Horse Ranch* to interview Mr. and Mrs. Holly, after receiving news that Cody was lost at the North Pole. The world press knew that without Cody, Santa would be grounded.

"Do not fear. Cody is a very curious and sometimes mischievous horse. He likes to explore his surroundings and is always on the hunt for treats. I may have spoiled him just a little bit, but he will show up," said Mr. Holly.

Meantime, back at Santa's Village, Cody plodded down Santa Clause Lane through the snow looking for adventure. He raised his head high and sniffed the air. Could it be? There was a smell of oatmeal cookies drifting through the swirling snowflakes. He followed the scent past the elf dormitory, school, and recreation center.

Then he spotted a round building shaped like a giant Christmas cookie, where the wonderful smell was coming from—Mrs. Claus's Bakery. A chocolate chip chimney sent puffs of white smoke blended with the aroma of oatmeal cookies into the air.

He trotted up to the bakery and peeked in a frosty window. Inside, Cody saw Santa's elves baking trays of Christmas cookies. They were singing a song to the tune of, "Are you sleeping?"

"Christmas cookies   *Christmas cookies*

Yum yum yum   *yum yum yum*

Baking Christmas cookies   *Baking Christmas cookies*

Yum yum yum   *yum yum yum"*

Cody nickered softly and his long tongue licked the window in anticipation of tasting a few of Mrs. Claus's delicious oatmeal cookies. Mrs. Claus stood next to a large round table surrounded by sacks of flour, sugar, oats, mixing bowls, rolling pin and cookie dough.

She wore a long red dress with a white trimmed collar. She had silver hair, deep blue eyes, rosy cheeks and a happy smile. She gazed over her clear spectacles and beamed with pride, as she watched the elves place the Christmas oatmeal cookies on cooling racks.

Cody watched intently, as the elves pushed the silver carts filled with cookies into a cooling room located on the north side of Mrs. Claus's bakery. He cantered around the building and spotted the trays of warm cookies cooling. He stepped inside the open doorway and looked around. There were no elves, just trays of cookies. He picked up one of them with his lips and was mesmerized by the tasty goodness. He ate one, then another, and another and another. Soon, the cookie trays were empty and Cody was sated. With his tummy full, he now wanted to find a warm place to take a nap. He slowly plodded to the north and peered across the barren land and shivered.

Santa and Alfred entered Mrs. Claus's bakery and explained that Cody was missing and if he wasn't found soon, there would not be enough horse power to pull Santa's sleigh full of toys.

Mrs. Claus gasped and the elves stopped singing and dancing. There was dead silence in the bakery. "Where do you think he could be? What happens if you cannot find him in time to help pull your sleigh," she asked?

"There will be no Christmas. There will be no toys for the boys and girls of the world," Santa said sadly.

Elf Jimmy came running through the bakery yelling, "Santa, Mrs. Claus, come quickly. They're gone! They're gone! All of the oatmeal cookies are gone!"

"Don't fret Jimmy. I think I know what happened to my oatmeal cookies," giggled Mrs. Claus. They hurriedly followed Jimmy to the cooling room.

The empty oatmeal cookie trays were scattered on the floor. They followed a trail of cookie crumbs to the open outside door. There in the fresh snow was a set of horse tracks heading due north toward the frozen tundra. The tracks were almost completely filled with snow and were disappearing rapidly.

"If Cody left the village and headed into the tundra he could be lost forever," cried Mrs. Claus. Alfred stared across the snowy frozen landscape of the forbidden tundra. Tears streamed down his rosy cheeks. "What can we do? There is no food, water, or shelter in the tundra," he whimpered.

Santa raised his arm and placed his finger on his nose and said, "I have a plan to find him. First, sound the elf alarm and ask everyone to be on the lookout for Cody. Then notify the *tundra snowmobile patrol* to search the tundra to the north, the direction of Cody's hoof prints. Buddy, Bobby, Copper and Zip should be finished at the harness shop, so text Tabitha and have her join us here. We will begin the search of my village as soon as

Tabitha and the horses arrive. Alfred, Twitter the Associated Press and advise them that Cody is still lost despite our efforts to find him. Quickly now, we only have fourteen hours left before my sleigh full of toys must be in the air. *You must all believe in the magic of Christmas.*"

Santa's plan went into effect quickly. Tabitha received the text message from Alfred. She hurriedly collected the horses from the harness shop and they joined Santa at the bakery. The snowmobile patrols could be heard zooming across the tundra. The horses lifted their heads and whinnied to their lost friend, hoping to hear a response, but there was none. Their calls echoed across the icy plains and fell into the deep chasms beyond.

"We must find Cody by 1 p.m. Each of you my equine friends must have at least eight hours of sleep before we start our journey. It is now 7 a.m. We have just six hours to find Cody," said Santa.

Santa, Mrs. Claus, Tabitha, Alfred and the horses searched for Cody throughout Santa's Village to no avail. It appeared that Cody had wandered out onto the frozen tundra of the North Pole. It was 10 a.m. when the small group reassembled at the bakery. Time was running out.

Santa's phone rang to the tune of jingle bells and flashed the name Elf Jamie. Mrs. Claus and Tabitha held their breath. Elf Jamie was the leader of the *tundra snowmobile patrol.* Santa answered the phone and spoke quietly to Jamie. He slowly nodded his head and said, "Thank you Jamie." The horses danced nervously. Tabitha waited to hear Santa tell them that Jamie had found Cody. Mrs. Claus looked over her spectacles and said, "Well, Santa?"

"They have called off the search in the tundra for Cody."

Buddy, Bobby, Copper and Zip lifted their heads high and sent whinnies of pain across the North Pole. Tabitha fell to the ground sobbing tears that melted the snow. Alfred hugged Santa's leg and wept. Mrs. Claus removed her glasses and dabbed her eyes with her apron. It was a heartbreaking moment at Santa's Village.

"Wait! This could only mean that Cody is still in the village. Surely, the tundra snowmobilers would have found him if he was nearby on the tundra. He could not have gone far with his tummy full of cookies," said Santa gleefully.

"Yes, said Buddy. Cody always takes a nap after he eats." "He must have found a place to lie down," said Zip.

"We are not looking for a tall horse. We are looking for a fat horse," laughed Santa.

A picture of Cody burst onto the screens of face book, smart phones and I pads. Everyone was tweeting and instant messaging at once. There were millions of children watching Christmas movies on SNN (Santa News Network). The devastating news flashed across the screens – *"Snowmobile patrols ends search for Cody. Brave horse feared forever lost in tundra among mountains of jagged ice"*

Then another message appeared on the screens from Santa Claus. "The search for Cody does not end. You must *believe* we will find our friend. I will soar through the skies above, always guided by the hand of love."

There was hope, despair and lots of prayers for the safe return of Cody throughout the world. Parents held their children tightly and whispered, "*You must believe in the magic of Christmas! Cody will be found and the horses from the Happy Horse Ranch in Lexington, Michigan, USA will rescue Christmas.*

Chapter 11

Cody stood staring out at the frozen tundra as shivers went up and down his spine.   He faced a terrain encrusted with deep snow and jagged ice as far as the eye could see. The wind whistled around his ankles and he stomped nervously in the snow.

"I certainly can't find a place to take a nap out there. I don't want to have to sleep in a snow cave. I think I will go back to the reindeer barn and find a warm stall and take a rest. I am anxious to try that red and green glittering bedding. Besides, I had better get back with Copper, Zip, Bobby, Buddy and Santa. They are probably wondering where I am."

Cody wandered back toward the reindeer barn, trudging through the snow behind the elf recreation center, school and dormitory.   He stopped and gazed in the window of the recreation center. The elves were playing a variety of board games, building tinker toys, coloring the horse pictures in the *Happy Horse Ranch* coloring book, playing ping-pong and watching the Santa News Network. Tunes of children Christmas songs could be heard through the windows. Cody meandered on his way, full of the spirit of Christmas as well as a tummy full of Mrs. Claus's oatmeal cookies.

He decided to stop and see what was being taught in elf school. There were rows of benches trimmed in candy cane stripes. The elves were all seated quietly listening to the professor, who stood in front of a large blackboard holding a pointer. There was a picture of a reindeer on the board.

The professor was wearing a red and green tweed jacket with gold buttons, a bright red turtle neck sweater, royal blue slacks and shiny black boots. His deep set dark brown eyes were filled with knowledge and his mouth formed an unending smile. The professor's dark brown hair covered the tips of his curved ears.

"Today's lesson is on *Rangifer tarandus* – the reindeer," said the professor. The students clapped their hands and cheered. The air was filled with excitement. This was their favorite subject.

The elves listened intently, as they readied paper and pencil to take notes.

"Reindeer are approximately 64" to 81" in length and weighs from 180 to 350 pounds. They vary in height from 33" to 59" at the shoulder. Their brown fur coat is made up of two layers of hair. The first layer is a dense wooly undercoat covered with a second longer overcoat with hollow air-filled hair, which keeps them warm. Both the male and female reindeer grow large antlers with sharp points. They have large flat razor-edged hooves so they can easily walk on the ice and snow. Santa's reindeer are considerably larger than average," he continued.

Cody wanted to hear more, but with a belly full of cookies he just wanted a warm stall and a nap. He slowly made his way behind the elves empty dormitory to the rear of Santa's reindeer barn. It was such a welcome site.

He whinnied his arrival to the other horses, but they did not answer. There was a sign on the back door of the barn which read *Reindeer Entrance Only.* Cody trotted to the front entrance of the barn and pushed the large green button on the white post with his nose and the sliding doors glided open.

Cody walked past the stalls of Dasher, Dancer, Prancer, Vixon, Comet, Cupid, Donner and Blitzen. They were fast asleep and did not elevate an antler when he pulled another flake of alfalfa down from the hay loft above their heads. After eating a few bites he continued to walk down the row of reindeer stalls.

He stood at the end stall and stared down in amazement at Rudolph the Red Nose Reindeer. He was much larger than the other reindeer and had such a sleek brown coat. His white chest marking accented his beautiful shaped face and hefty set of gleaming antlers. There was a low grunt and Rudolph opened his eyes. They were warm friendly eyes that reflected a soft red glimmer from his red nose. He looked at Cody affectionately and nodded his head slightly. Cody nickered softly back to let Rudolph know that he knew exactly what was expected of him.

"I will use all of my might to make certain Santa's sleigh maintains a good height," he whispered. Rudolph closed his eyes and snuggled back in the sparkling red and green stall bedding. Rudolph knew that the horses would indeed *rescue Christmas*.

Cody glanced around the barn and again whinnied for his friends. The barn was empty, except for the reindeer, which were all fast asleep. Then, on the opposite side of the barn, Cody spotted an empty stall with the same glittering bedding and a bucket with fresh water. The sign on the wall read *Guest Stall Only*.

Cody slid open the door latch with his nose, dropped to his knees and rolled over in the glittering bedding. He took a deep breath and snorted, sending red and green sprinkles far into the air. He fell asleep quickly and entered a dream world where there were stacks and stacks of Mrs. Claus's homemade oatmeal cookies.

"Come with me everyone. I think I know where we will find Cody. We searched the entire village, except for one place. We did not return to the barn. He could have returned to the barn by walking behind the elf complex and that is why we didn't see him," said Santa.

The air was filled with hope and excitement, as the small search party made their way back to the reindeer barn. Santa pushed the large green button on the fence post and the barn doors opened wide. The soft sound of contented snoring drifted throughout the barn.

"That sounds like Cody all right," nickered Bobby.

"Follow me," Zip whinnied.

The horses trotted into the barn, past the stalls with Santa's sleeping reindeer, and several partially-eaten bales of alfalfa lying on the floor. They abruptly stopped in front of Rudolph's stall, raised their heads and sent forth powerful whinnies. They shifted their ears forward and listened intently. Then they heard a contented snoring sound coming from a guest stall located on the opposite side of the barn.

"I believe we have found Cody," laughed Santa.

Whinnies of joy, snickers and nickers resonated throughout Santa's reindeer barn, as the search party stared at Cody stretched out in the sparkling bedding of the guest stall.

Cody lifted his head, nickered to his friends, and bounded to his feet. He gave a big shake, sending green and red sparkles all over everyone.

Santa brushed the sparkles from his beard and laughingly declared, "Let's get ready to *rescue Christmas.*"

The world let out a sigh of relief when word was received from Santa's communication center that Cody had been found at last.

Santa's viral message read: *Cody has been found, sleeping in a stall, safe and sound. He is suffering from a slight tummy ache caused by eating too many of Mrs. Claus's oatmeal cookies. All horses are now eating a nutritious meal of hay and grain. They will rest in their stalls prior to being harnessed to my sleigh full of toys. There has not been time to practice take off and landings. Boys and girls, remember to put out milk, cookies, kitty treats and carrots. Believe! Signed: Santa*

The news media was wild with speculation. They pointed out that Santa's message did not mention if Cody's tummy ache would keep him from pulling Santa's sleigh. His message also said there had not been time to practice take off and landings. What if Santa's sleigh crashed on takeoff, scattering the toys for the boys and girls of the world across the North Pole?

Could the world really expect five *rescue horses* from different backgrounds and breeds to make a perfectly coordinated take off from the North Pole on the first try? After all, this would be the first time they have been harnessed together. Journalists speculated that lifting Santa and his sleigh full of toys into the snowy sky would not be easy,

Santa tucked the horses into their stalls with an ample supply of rich green hay, a big scoop of fresh oats, and a bucket of fresh water. "You must all eat and get plenty of rest. We start our long journey in a few hours. You must be well rested to circle the world, bringing so much joy with my sleigh full of toys." The horses whinnied and pawed the green and red sparkles on the floor of their stalls, creating a blizzard of excitement. Tabitha and Alfred climbed each stall gate and gave each horse a warm hug around their necks.

"We love each of you so much," said Tabitha. "Yes, we do, and thank you for spreading so much love and happiness around the world," said Alfred. Tears of joy trickled down the elves rosy cheeks and were gently licked away by the horses. Santa turned his back and dabbed a tear from his eyes, amid the soft nickers and neighs.

Suddenly, there was a rustling sound from the hayloft, as sprinkles of hay floated down, followed by a small thump. There in the midst of a clump of alfalfa stood Jaboozala. "Don't leave without me," she meowed.

The horses whinnied, the elves fell down laughing, and Santa let out a roaring laugh from deep within his belly. Santa picked up Jaboozala and placed her on his shoulder. He gave her a big hug. The barn rocked with whinnying, laughing, Ho! Ho! Ho!, and loud purring. "You are going to ride high in the sky seated by my side tonight, Jaboozala," laughed Santa.

"Do any of you have any questions before you begin your flight into the night," asked Santa?

The horses talked among themselves for a few moments. Tails were swishing and their heads were bobbing up and down in agreement. Zip stepped forward and asked, "Can Tabitha and Alfred come with us tonight?"

Santa was taken completely by surprise at the request. He rubbed his chin in deep thought. For a moment, he seemed to be rendered speechless. Then his eyes twinkled and he cheerfully said, "Tabitha and Alfred will be on my sleigh. Now you must eat and sleep, my friends, for on your strength the *rescue of Christmas* now depends."

The rhythmic sounds of munching hay soon gave way to deep breathing, as the horses fell into a deep sleep. Santa would call upon their strength and energy in a few short hours to *rescue Christmas.*

Chapter 12

*T*he world held its breath as the final few hours ticked away before the horses from the *Happy Horse Ranch* attempted their take off from the North Pole, lifting Santa and his sleigh full of toys into the sky.

There would not be a second chance! If the horses failed to fly on their first try, Santa's toys would be scattered across the frozen tundra. There would be no toys for the boys and girls of the world. There would only be tears and sadness.

Then the airways crackled with a message from Santa. The message read; "Boys and girls, moms and dads, you must *believe in me, the horses, and the magic of Christmas.*"

The grocery stores quickly sold out of apples and carrots. Extra milk was purchased and the cookie shelves were soon barren. Yes, even the kitty treats had been sold out. Excitement rose, as dads placed heaps of carrots, apples and kitties treats on their rooftops next to the chimneys. Moms helped their children place cookies and milk on the kitchen tables for Santa, Tabitha and Alfred.

Satellites from Outer Space honed in on the North Pole, anxiously watching and waiting for the moment Santa and his sleigh full of toys lifted skyward. Christmas trees twinkled silently with their outstretched arms waiting to receive Santa's presents.

Fires were extinguished in the homes with fireplaces. The ashes were removed and Christmas stockings were hung from the mantels. The homes without a fireplace left a door or window unlocked so Santa could deliver his toys.

Meanwhile, at the *Happy Horse Ranch*, Mr. and Mrs. Holly were decorating the barn to welcome home Bobby, Buddy, Cody, Copper, Zip and Jaboozala. Thousands of Christmas cards, letters and e-mails flooded the mail box and the computer Inbox of the *Happy Horse Ranch* from well wishers around the world. Mrs. Holly printed the e-mails on festive red and green paper and Mr. Holly carried three bushel baskets of happiness to the barn.

Silver garland weaved and snaked through the rafters and across the stall doors. The cards and colorful e-mails were strung from the garland and danced in glee. Large red stockings were filled with peppermints, carrots and apples and hung on each stall door. Mrs. Holly put Jaboozala's favorite kitty treats in her special dish and placed it on a hay bale high in the hay mound. A gigantic green banner with large red lettering was hung across the peak of the barn. The banner read "WELCOME HOME BOBBY, BUDDY, CODY, COPPER, ZIP AND JABOOZALA."

Even though preparations were already underway to receive them home, their long flight with Santa Claus had not yet begun. There were many challenges ahead for the horses of the *Happy Horse Ranch*.

Santa was also making last minute preparations for his Christmas flight. He studied the latest weather reports from his smartphone. There were strong wind warnings for the Rocky Mountains, rain in San Francisco, and warm temperatures in Las Vegas. Heavy snow was predicted across the Midwest and the Northeast coast, and blizzard conditions with strong cross winds at the Straits of Mackinaw, which separate the Lower and Upper Peninsula of Michigan.

Santa studied the weather report and slowly rubbed his snowy white beard. The part of the report that concerned him the most was the forecast for the Straits of Mackinaw, which was in his direct flight path to reach the rest of the United States. "The horses will have to be extra strong to fight their way through a blizzard and vicious cross winds, where Michigan's Lake Huron and Lake Michigan battled for dominance. "I have complete confidence in them. They will do it. After all, Michigan is their home state and the Mackinaw Bridge is only 285 miles from the *Happy Horse Ranch*," he thought to himself.

Santa continued on, tromping through the snowy streets of his village making his next stop at the toy factory. Dozens and dozens of elves were busy putting the last minute touches on thousands of toys, sorting games, packaging dolls and assembling bicycles, scooters, skateboards and such. Children's Christmas songs echoed happily through the workshop.

I-phones, I-pads, I-pods, cell phones and smartphones were being carefully wrapped in the electronic department. The aisleways buzzed with activity as elves scurried back and forth with presents wrapped in colorful paper and adorned with large bows, all ready to pack on Santa's sleigh. A large banner hung from the ceiling that read "ELF POWER."

Santa smiled broadly as he passed by row after row of presents that would bring so much laughter, giggles and screams of joy to the many children who did *believe* in Christmas. He stopped and thanked the many elves that helped him make the *magic of Christmas* come true. Soon there were dozens of elves surrounding Santa, cheering and shouting "Merry Christmas!" They rushed forward and gave Santa a group *elf hug.* Santa laughed merrily and shouted above the din; "Ho! Ho! Ho! Merry Christmas."

Multiple conveyor belts churned their way to the rear of the toy factory, all stopping at Santa's sleigh-loading dock. The colorful presents were stacked and sorted with children names and scanned by GPS to insure proper delivery. The elves danced and sang, as they went about their happy work.

Santa opened his bag and pulled out a long computerized list of children names that were on the **Naughty and Nice List.** There were only a few naughty children on Santa's list. He reviewed these carefully to see if they would receive presents for Christmas.

The first name on the list was Billy in Fort Worth, Texas, age eight. Santa learned that Billy had teased the girls in his class and made them cry. Santa read a note from his teacher, who informed him that since Billy saw Santa at the Fort Worth Shopping Mall he has been a good boy. The teacher recommended that Billy be removed from Santa's naughty list, so Santa switched Billy to his nice list.

Next on the naughty list was Sarah, age seven, and Josh, age six. Santa learned that they argued with each other, didn't obey their parents and would cry when it was bedtime. Santa received a text message from the mother of Sarah and Josh that read: " I explained to the children about the *magic of Christmas* and your Naughty and Nice List. They have changed their behavior and are now great kids. Please remove them from you naughty list. Santa cheerfully moved Sarah and Josh to the nice list.

Then, Santa read about Tommy, age nine, from Bangor, Maine, who was a *bully.* Tommy pushed smaller kids around, started fights, and his classmates were afraid of him. Santa sadly removed Tommy's presents from the loading dock. "Maybe he will be a better boy next year," he sighed.

Santa read the names of the remaining children on the naughty list and found that these boys and girls had changed their behavior. They were joyfully added to the nice list. Their naughty behavior had been changed by the *magic of Christmas.*

"Ho! Ho! Ho! Bring out my sleigh," Santa exclaimed. Cheers and merriment ricocheted from the toy factory throughout Santa's Village. All of the elves started to sing; "Here comes Santa Claus." Santa's snowy little village was filled with warmth and love.

It was time to bring out Santa's sleigh and fill it with toys.

Chapter 13

NOAA (the National Oceanic and Atmospheric Administration) sent an emergency weather warning to the sheriffs of Mackinaw, Cheboygan, and Emmet counties. The Michigan State Police, chiefs of police for the cities of Mackinaw, St. Ignace and the Mackinaw Bridge Authority also received the same warning.

Blizzard conditions and strong winds, with gusts up to 60 miles-per-hour, would prevail across the Straits of Mackinaw from 8 p.m. until midnight on Christmas Eve. Air traffic control notified commercial air traffic of storm conditions reaching an elevation of 5,000 feet above the icy waters at the straits.

The Northern Michigan Emergency Weather Operations Center was activated to make preparations for the looming blizzard with gale force winds. A meeting was held and each county agreed to combine all of their manpower and equipment to fight the fury of Mother Nature.

The sheriff departments, Mackinaw and St. Ignace police departments and the Michigan State Police would patrol both sides off the bridge, ready to assist stranded motorists. Emergency shelters were opened at St. Ignace and Mackinaw High Schools. EMS Units stood ready to respond to any medical emergencies. Fire Departments were prepared to offer assistance or react to any emergency. Three veterinary doctors also volunteered to help.

The snow started to cover the landscape across Northern Michigan with a white blanket of cold. The north winds whistled in intensity, blowing the happiness from the dancing snowflakes. Snow plows challenged the forces of nature with their huge blades of iron, as they struggled to keep the roads clear of drifting snow. A blizzard travel advisory was posted for I-75 and the Mackinaw Bridge.

Meanwhile, at Santa's Village, it was time for Santa's elves to load his sleigh. Dozens of elves gathered at the loading platform. The presents were stacked on the platform according to zip codes along Santa's flight plan. Children's names and address were checked for accuracy. Photos from Google Earth told Santa if the house did or did not have a chimney.

The elves danced and sang, as they waited for the magic moment. Suddenly, there was silence. The clock in Santa's Village square gonged eight times. All eyes turned to the red and white candy cane hangar behind the toy factory, which housed Santa's sleigh. The doors opened slowly and the sleigh coasted down the small grad, magically stopping at the loading platform.

The sleigh was bright red with deep green-colored front and rear seats. Santa's seat had a high back, with a heated seat with lumbar support. The front of the sleigh curved back above the dashboard. There was a special heated compartment beneath the dash that would keep Jaboozala warm between stops. Elf-size seat belts were mounted to the back seat. The curved black runners had been waxed for smooth rooftop landings. The words MERRY CHRISTMAS appeared in large lettering on both sides of the sleigh.

The joyous group of elves cheered and applauded. There were hugs and tears of joy, as they celebrated the final hour of their 364 days of hard work. Tabitha and Alfred were hoisted in the air. Her happy meow could not be heard as Santa lifted Jaboozala high above his head shouting, "Ho! Ho! Ho! Lets load the presents and go!" The *rescue of Christmas* was about to get underway.

Mrs. Claus dashed to Santa's side with a thermos of hot chocolate and a package of oatmeal cookies. "Take these with you for a little snack on the way. You never know, you may get delayed," she said. She gave Santa a warm hug.

"I am so proud of you, Tabitha and Alfred. Just think, you are the first elves in the history of the world to ride with Santa. Not only are you the first, but you are forever part of *A Christmas Rescue,* with the horses of the *Happy Horse Ranch.*" She stooped down and gave each of them a hug. She then removed Jaboozala from Santa's shoulder and gave her a hug. "You, Jaboozala, will be the first cat ever to be on Santa's lap," she laughed, as she put a package of kitty treats in Santa's pocket. There was more clapping and shouts of joy.

"Tabitha and Alfred, go quickly to the reindeer barn and bring the horses. Tell them the boys and girls of the world are depending upon them. Now is the time to show the world the might of the horse."

The horses were standing in their stalls, well-rested, appetites sated and full of nervous energy. They stood waiting to begin the adventure of a lifetime. Tabitha and Alfred came running down the aisle.

"It's time to go! Santa is waiting. Jaaboozala is waiting. The children are waiting!" Alfred yelled excitedly.

"Yes, it is time to *rescue Christmas*," shouted Tabitha.

The horses whinnied and danced with excitement. There was a blizzard of green and red stall bedding bits as the horses rushed from their stalls.

Suddenly, there was a flurry of grunts and snorts coming from Santa's reindeer. The horse's large eyes widened, as they saw Rudolph, Dasher,

Dancer, Prancer, Vixon, Comet, Cupid, Donner and Blitzen standing in their stalls on wobbly legs. They were still feeling the symptoms of the reindeer flu, but they still came out of their stalls and stood in a circle around the horses. Rudolph's nose casted a reduced red glow. He stood in front of Zip, whose nose was shining brightly.

"Zip, we want to thank you and the horses from the *Happy Horse Ranch* for rescuing Christmas. We wish each of you a very Merry Christmas and God Speed." He touched noses with Zip and there was an explosion of sparkles.

"I wanted to recharge your nose one more time, so your might will shine through the night. Now the children will sing, *Zip, the red nose horsee, instead of Rudolph, the red nose reindeer,*" he snorted.

There was laughter, hugs, grunts and snorts, as the horses and reindeer exchanged well wishes. A new friendship between *Equs ferus caballus* and *Rangifer tarandus* would forever be a part of Christmas from now on.

"Pick me up, Zip!" Tabitha hollered. Zip lowered his head and she scrambled up his nose, through his thick mane and onto his back. She leaned forward with her arms wrapped around his huge neck and hugged him tightly. He quietly nickered.

"How about me, Cody?" Alfred yelled. "Let me help," said Bobby, as he reached down and picked Alfred up by his shirt collar, dangled him in the air, and dropped him on Cody's back.

The reindeer and horses snorted and snickered. Alfred laughed and shouted, "Getty up, it's time to go."

Zip and Tabitha led the procession of horses out of the barn into the frosty air, amid cheers from the reindeer. They followed the path of twinkling lights that would take them to the loading platform behind Santa's toy shop. Large snowflakes tumbled from the moonlit sky and joyful Christmas songs welcomed the horses. The final presents were being stacked high on Santa's sleigh.

"Welcome my friends. On you, Christmas depends. I will often say whoa. There will be rooftops so many and landings a plenty. No sound should we make so the children don't wake. The milk I shall drink and cookies I'll munch. The carrots are yours to savor and crunch. There will be plenty of hay tucked away in the sleigh. Tabitha and Alfred have special treats baked only for elves to eat. My pocket has yummies for Jaboozala's tummy."

"As we get underway here what awaits you my horses with sleigh; Miles and miles of green forests in a blanket of white waving at you on Christmas Eve night. We will zoom over mountain tops covered in snow that give way to the heat of the deserts below. Cities of all sizes will twinkle afar, as we whiz overhead dancing with stars. Shimmering lakes with chunks of ice on the land will be left behind for glittering sand.   Landing on rooftops, some flat and some steep, will not make it easy to stay on your feet. All of these things I mention so you will know nothing can stop you, not mountains or snow. Remember the children whose hearts are so happy, waiting to get up and start unwrapping."

The North Pole quaked in merriment with shouts of "Go Zip Go! Go Zip Go!" Zip reared up on his hind legs, stretched is neck and head skyward, and let out a massive whinny. Red-colored sound waves from his glowing nose radiated skyward. The other horses whinnied, bucked, reared up and snorted. The large clock bonged once. It was 8:30 p.m., almost time to go.

"Hurry now and line up for your harnesses. We must be underway by 9 p.m." Bobby and Cody backed up to the loading platform in front of Santa's sleigh, followed by Buddy and Copper. Zip then whirled around creating a whirlwind of snow, and he said to the horses, "Are you ready to go?" The horses stomped and nickered. Zip stood in front of Buddy and Copper and nodded to Santa.

Elf Henry and his harness makers scampered in, on, and underneath the horses putting on shiny black harnesses that were fitted on each horse and connected one to the other.   When they were finished there was a team of five waiting for Santa to get in and drive.

Elves scampered back and forth, hurriedly putting last minute presents on the sleigh. They checked the harnesses connections, sprayed the horses with de-icer spray, set Santa's GPS, and put a fresh coat of wax on the runners of Santa's sleigh for easy take offs and landing. In the luggage compartment of the sleigh they packed extra bags of Magic Flying Powder and an emergency winter survival kit.

The final task on the flight list was to spray the horses with Magic Flying Powder. Elf Henry held a large hose that was connected to a barrel of the powder. He turned on the motor and a fine spray shot from the end of the hose, covering the horses with a coating of the magic substance. The horses danced and whinnied, barely able to keep their feet on the ground.

Tabitha and Alfred climbed into the back seat of the sleigh and waved to the cheering elves of Santa's Village. Then Santa climbed aboard with Jaboozala on his shoulder, picked up the reins and shouted, "Merry Christmas to all and to all a good night!"

Through the cheers, whinnies, snorts, and shouts of joy a small voice was heard. "Wait Santa," yelled Mrs. Claus. She came through the crowd of elves on the platform waving a small red coat with white fur trim and a red Santa hat in her hand.

"This is for Jaboozala. Not only will it keep the cold from her fur, but if you listen carefully, you may hear her purr." She put the coat and hat on a willing Jaboozala to the laugher of Santa, the elves and the nickers of horses. She kissed Santa on the cheek and said, "A Merry Christmas to each of you and to the entire world."

Santa jiggled the reins and the horses moved slowly, pulling Santa and his sleigh full of toys down Santa Claus Lane, heading for the North Pole runway.

Chapter 14

*T*he sleigh glided smoothly down Santa Claus Lane, pulled for the first time in history by *horse power*. The sleigh was trailed by Mrs. Claus and all of the elves in Santa's Village. Even Santa's reindeer left the reindeer barn on wobbly legs to watch the horses from the *Happy Horse Ranch* lift Santa and his sleigh full of toys into the sky.

Tabitha and Alfred hugged each other, as they listened to the brass bells jingle on the horses. Jaboozala sat on Santa's shoulder, watching her barn buddies walking in perfect step. Santa held the reins firmly, as they approached the snowy runway located next to the Jet Sled hangar. He positioned the sleigh, pointing it due south.

"Fasten your seat belts and get ready for lift off," said Santa. He tucked Jaboozala inside his coat. A pair of green eyes and pointed ears peeked out of Santa's coat by his neck.

Santa said a short prayer: "Dear God, send us on our way to deliver my toys to the children, as the Three Wise Men did for your son, Jesus Christ, on this day, many centuries ago. Let the world celebrate the reason for this joyous season. Amen."

"Zip, Copper, Buddy, Cody and Bobby when the village clock strikes the first stroke of nine you will gallop at full speed and not look behind. At the stroke of eight you heads will no longer be straight. You will raise your heads high ready to fly." The horse nickered and danced, anxious to be given this chance. It was now only seconds away to start *a Christmas rescue.*

"Ho! Ho! Ho! It's off to *rescue Christmas* we shall go."

The silence was deafening, as Mrs. Claus, the village elves, and Santa's reindeer held their breath. Then it happened! The clock in the village gonged the first stroke of nine, and it suddenly looked like the horses had been shot from a cannon. They raced faster and faster toward the quickly-approaching end of the snowy runway. The clocked gonged twice…three times… four… five… six…seven and eight.

"Lift your heads high!" shouted Santa. The clock gonged for the ninth time. It was a magical sight to behold—five magnificent horses from the *Happy Horse Ranch* lifting Santa and his sleigh into the sky pushing the snowflakes aside with their powerful strides. The silhouetted horses seemed to be prancing on the face of the glowing moon. There was cheering and shouts of joy from below. The loudspeakers in the village burst into song. All of Santa's helpers began singing. *"Here Comes Santa Claus."*

Santa circled his village below led by Zip, with his nose brightly aglow. Mrs. Claus and the elves cheered wildly, as Santa's sleigh disappeared into the night.

The toy deliveries started in the far regions of Northern Canada. Santa coached and encouraged the horses on making smooth rooftop landings. "Remember, lift your heads up to rise, heads straight ahead to stay level on our flight path and drop your heads down to land." There were a couple of big thuds on the snowy rooftops, here and there, that would require a bit of shingle repair, as the horses practiced their landings.

The landings on rooftops and the ground rapidly improved, and soon the horses were crisscrossing the Upper Peninsula of Michigan filled with confidence. Santa brought his sleigh down for a landing on the football field of Sault St. Marie High School. "It is time to take a short break to rest and eat some hay, my friends," said Santa. The horses whinnied in agreement. Tabitha and Alfred opened the hay compartment on the sleigh and took each horse a flake of green alfalfa. They were soon filled with energy. They snorted, danced and stomped their feet between the goal posts, as they waited patiently for Santa, Tabitha, Alfred and Jaboozala to finish their snacks. When they were finished eating, Santa got an updated weather report for the Mackinaw Bridge from his smartphone. There were now blizzard conditions blocking the path between the upper and lower peninsulas of Michigan.

Santa removed a bag from under the front seat of his sleigh marked **Snow Goggles.** He stood next to Zip and held up a pair for the horses to see. The goggles covered both eyes and had straps that buckled behind the head. "We will soon be flying through a blizzard over the Straits of Mackinaw. These goggles will give extra protection for your eyes. Bend your head down, Zip, and we will show the others how handsome you look with goggles," said Santa. Zip dropped his head and Santa placed the extra large goggles across his eyes and buckled the straps behind his head. Zip turned his head for the others to see. The horses whinnied laughter of approval.

Tabitha and Alfred removed the goggles from Santa's bag and sorted them according to size. They climbed from the sleigh onto Bobby and Cody's backs. They jumped from horse to horse and fitted the goggles. Santa climbed into his sleigh and put on a pair himself. Tabitha and Alfred found two pairs of extra small goggles and promptly put them on. Tabitha checked the bag and found a pair marked "tiny." Jaboozala meowed and held her head up high, while Tabitha fitted her goggles too.

"Ho! Ho! Ho! Let's go! We will not be stopped by a little snow."

The horses pulled the sleigh at break neck speed down the length of the football field and soared into the sky. Santa followed the I-75 highway toward the Mackinaw Bridge. The weather changed from soft snowflakes to a combination of blinding snow and sleet. Santa opened the small heated compartment under the dash of the sleigh and Jaboozala jumped inside, eager to get out of the blizzard's wrath. Tabitha and Alfred climbed from the rear seat to the front and huddled under the dash to keep from getting blown away by the howling wind and blinding snow.

"We have one mile to go, according to my GPS. The bridge should be directly in front of us. Our altitude is too low to fly over the bridge. You must fly across it."

"Copper is losing his strength. Hang on Copper! We are being pulled down," Zip whinnied.

Copper fought with all his might to stay upright in the ferocious winds and snow lashing both horse and sleigh. "Just because I am thirty-five-years-old does not mean that I can't pull my fair share," he whinnied. He mustered every ounce of strength from his small Arabian body. Inch by inch he slowly rose in place next to Buddy. He rubbed noses with Buddy, as the sleigh uprighted to a level position. "Way to go, Copper. You must *believe* in yourself," Santa yelled through the gale force winds. Copper nickered to Santa, but his nicker was carried away by the wind.

Suddenly the image of *Mighty Mac,* the longest suspension bridge in the Western Hemisphere, broke through the vicious blanket of snow and loomed in front of them. The bridge rose 551 feet above the Straits of Mackinaw, while the icy waters from Lake Huron and Lake Michigan battled below for supremacy.

"We cannot continue in this storm. Each of us must rest, and it is eight more miles across the bridge. I have sent an S.O.S (Save Our Santa) to the Emergency Operation Center at Mackinaw. Bobby, Cody, Buddy and Copper follow the courage of Zip. We must get my toys delivered before dawn," said Santa.

The horses glided between the Mighty Mac's mammoth pillars of concrete and steel. The red and green light that lit the bridge came dimly into view. "Keep your heads straight. When I tell you, lower your heads slightly down until you feel the deep snow on your hooves," Zip whinnied.

The railings on the bridge whizzed by, as Santa, sleigh and horses touched down smoothly in the deep snow on the crest of Mighty Mac.

"We will not be able to take off again in this heavy snow," said Bobby." The others joined in agreement.

"The deep snow, poor visibility and angry winds will keep us stranded on the crest of the Mackinaw Bridge," said a worried Cody.

"The snow is up to my belly and I am getting cold," said Copper.

"I feel the bridge swaying," Buddy added.

"Do not be alarmed. This bridge was built to sway back and forth thirty-five feet from east to west in strong winds." yelled Santa.

"You must *believe my friends*. You are rescuing Christmas. Even my reindeer would not have the strength to fight this blizzard. Zip, I commend you for your strength and lighting the way for us. Copper, you have shown great courage and determination in fighting this terrible storm. Buddy, Bobby, and Cody, you have the power and endurance to see that my toys are delivered," praised Santa.

Santa trudged through the blinding snow and wicked winds until he stood next to Zip. He wrapped his arms around Zip's huge neck and gave him a warm Santa hug. Zip nickered quietly, as his red nose became supercharged, illuminating the crest of *Mighty Mac* in a red glow. The winds immediately subsided and once again soft snow flakes drifted gently to the water below. The blizzard was over! There were whinnies of joy from the horses, cheers from Tabitha and Alfred, and a happy meow from Jaboozala.

"Santa, how are we going to be able to take off when the snow is up to the bellies of the horses," asked Tabitha?

"Do not fear, Tabitha. Look to the north and look to the south," said Santa.

The yellow flashing lights of mammoth snowplows headed toward Santa's sleigh. The plows created a whirlwind, as they pushed the deep snow through the cables of the bridge, sending tons of snow into the depths of the treacherous waters far below.

The law enforcement vehicles from three counties followed with flashing blue and red lights from St. Ignace to the north and the City of Mackinaw to the south. The two groups met at the crest of the bridge, amid the cheers from Santa, Tabitha and Alfred. The horses whinnied with excitement. They were filled with energy and anxious to get back into the sky.

The mayors of St. Ignace and Mackinaw climbed down from the snow plows and embraced Santa Claus. The snowplow drivers, police officers and firefighters hugged all the horses, Tabitha, Alfred and Jaboozala. Shouts of "Merry Christmas!" echoed across the bridge. Squeals, whinnies, and meows added to the joyful sounds of Christmas.

"We must get underway my friends. We have much work to do before daylight creeps across the land. Many thanks for clearing the bridge of snow and spreading the sand, so the horses won't slow down. We mustn't sit still with so many stockings to fill."

The horses shook the snow from their backs and lined up behind Zip. They were filled with nervous energy. Zip reared into the air, shooting red steam from his nose. The southern lanes of the bridge swayed slightly in the snow and wind. Tabitha and Alfred waved goodbye and yelled, "Merry Christmas!" to the crowd of rescuers. Jaboozala jumped into Santa's arms and wrapped her little paws around his warm neck and snuggled beneath his fluffy white beard. A pair of large green eyes peered through the white tufts of beard. The crowd laughed and cheered, "Go, Santa, Go!"

"Let's go my equine friends. We have many chimney stops, before this night ends. Light the way for us to see," Santa shouted to Zip. He turned and nodded his head to the other horses, who all whinnied in excitement. Santa's sleigh lunged forward and the crowd roared with cheers and shouts. Zip's glowing red nose lit up the runway to the sky as they all broke into a gallop at breakneck speed.

"Lift your heads to the sky," said Zip. The metal grates on the bridge roadway hummed a happy tune, as the horses and sleigh sped across them. Santa was lifted into the starry night sky above the Lower Peninsula of Michigan. The red and green lights on the *Mighty Mac* disappeared, engulfed in a blanket of white. The strong winds had disappeared into the heavens far above the Earth. Zip's red nose guided Santa and his sleigh from house to house along the frozen shoreline of Lake Huron.

"When do we get to Florida?" grumbled Cody. "I don't like blizzards," groaned Copper. "I will be happy when we go to Hawaii," nickered Bobby. I hear Southern California has warm weather, "Buddy added.

"Yes, it will be nice to visit some warm spots across the United States, but remember we are snow horses. There are thousands of children in the cold states who depend on Santa for warm coats and mittens. Besides, can you imagine how many of those nasty biting flies are around all year long in those states with hot weather?" Zip responded.

Santa joined the conversation between the horses. "I am so proud of each of you for rescuing Christmas. I picked you because of your strength, endurance, and your happiness. Think about the many children who are depending on us. You conquered the Mackinaw Bridge in a raging blizzard!" said Santa.

Tabitha and Alfred cheered, "Let's go! Let's go! Let's go!" The horses galloped with joy above the shoreline of Lake Huron. There were chants from the horses of "We are snow horses. Here we come, boys and girls. Hang on tight, Santa, and Merry Christmas to all!"

The horses raced across the starry sky of snow, landing on rooftops far below. Santa slid down the chimneys with ease and placed his presents under the trees.

There were many homes without chimneys, so Santa landed his sleigh on the ground and snuck his presents through the front door. He drank his milk, ate a cookie or two, and returned to his sleigh bringing carrots for the horses and kitty treats for Jaboozala. Once appetites were satisfied they were back in the sky.

Zip's bright red nose which lit the way was no more than a red pinprick disappearing into the sky. They crisscrossed the United States, going through deep snow, over mountain peaks, and across desert sands, bringing the promise of Christmas upon the land.

Chapter 16

*T*he dark sky started to lighten beyond the eastern horizon of Lake Huron. The Village of Lexington stood silently in the predawn hours. It had been decorated with twinkling lights, garland and Christmas trees. Large signs peppered the village that read "LEXINGTON, HOME OF THE HAPPY HORSE RANCH. THE HORSES THAT RESCUED CHRISTMAS!"

Crowds of onlookers lined the road to the *Happy Horse Ranch*. There were news media trucks with satellites dishes, cars, pickup trucks, tractors, ATV's, and snowmobiles. Everyone was waiting to get a glimpse of Santa and the horses that *rescued Christmas.*

Mr. and Mrs. Jolly spent the night inside the barn so they could welcome home their beloved horses and barn kitty. They slept under heavy quilts and blankets between the bales of hay.

"Do you think we will meet Santa, Alfred and Tabitha?" she asked. "I don't think so," answered Mr. Jolly. They both yawned and shortly fell asleep in the hay.

Crowds of people shined flashlights and spotlights into the sky, as dawn was breaking above the roof of the barn at the *Happy Horse Ranch*. Vehicle headlights pierced the drifts of snow in the darkened pastures.

Suddenly, as the sun peeked slightly above the horizon, there was a strong gust of wind that blew a blinding snow across the road, house, barn, and pastures of the *Happy Horse Ranch*. Visibility became zero, and when the wind stopped there was a hushed quiet.

Mr. and Mrs. Jolly awoke to the loud whinny of Bobby. Then there was nickering from the other horses. Jaboozala stretched on a bale of hay and meowed. Lying beneath her was a red Santa hat with a white tassel filled with kitty treats.

The horse's stockings were filled with carrots and peppermint candies, except for Cody's. His stocking was filled with oatmeal cookies. Copper and Buddy stood proudly waiting for breakfast. The Jollys saw a fading red glow coming from Zip's stall. They rushed to his stall and saw a dim red glow vanishing from his nose. Soon it was gone.

They rushed from the barn and looked to the northern sky. The fading stars twinkled , forming the letters:

'B   E   L   I   E   V   E'

About the Author

Fred Marengo was born and raised in Lexington, Michigan. It is still the quaint village nestled along the shores of Lake Huron that represents the best of "Small Town America."

Fred enlisted in the United States Marine Corps for a six year obligation, returning home to join the St. Clair Shores Police Department, where he served for twenty-nine years, retiring as Deputy Chief of Police.

Fred returned to his roots with his wife Susan and children Shannon and Adam. He fell in love with horses and penned his first book, "Second Chances - A Story of Love, Faith and Rescue" that has brought so much joy and hope to many readers across the country. Fred and Susan still reside in Lexington with their five rescue horses at the Happy Horse Ranch, along with their rescue kitties and a dog.

CPSIA information can be obtained at www.ICGtesting.com
Printed in the USA
BVOW06*1112051014

368420BV00006B/4/P